Good Fortune
in a Wrapping Cloth

By Joan Schoettler

Illustrated by Jessica Lanan

SHEN'S BOOKS

"Eomma, listen. Horses."
Ji-su pressed closer to her mother.
"Stay. Don't go to King Yongjo's court."

"It is an honor for me, and our family, to
sew *bojagi* for the royal household," Eomma
told her again. "The Sanguiwon master
searches for the finest seamstresses. He saw
one of my *bojagi* at the market and chose me.
I must go to Hanyang."

Ji-su wished Uncle had used an old cloth instead of one of Eomma's *bojagi* to wrap oranges he sold that day at the market.

"My dear daughter, be strong like bamboo." Eomma had used the same words after Ji-su's father left to go fishing and never returned. She handed Ji-su a *bojagi*-covered gift. "Open this after I leave. Wrapping a package with a *bojagi*, we send good luck to the person — blessings and wishes of happiness, health, and good fortune."

"I want to go with you," Ji-su whispered. Her stomach churned like she'd eaten a sour apple.

"I can't take you." Eomma dropped the cloth covering her head so no one would see her face. "The palace will be my home now." Tears ran along Ji-su's cheeks as she watched Eomma disappear beyond the curve in the road.

Unfolding the *bojagi*, Ji-su felt her mother's *bok* in the patterns covering her lap. She unlocked the iron clasp on Eomma's old box. Opening it, Ji-su touched each of Eomma's seven close companions: a needle, thread, a thimble, a ruler, a pair of scissors, a small iron called an *indoo*, and an iron with a bowl to hold charcoal called a *darimi*.

"Eomma promised to teach me to stitch *bojagi* when I turned eleven," Ji-su said to Gomo, her old aunt, "but now she's gone."

Gomo wiped Ji-su's tears. "When the king commands something, it must be done."

"Someday I'm going to sew a *bojagi* as fine as Eomma's, then the Sanguiwon master will choose me too." Ji-su opened a basket with fabric scraps. "Will you teach me?"

Ji-su hurried to the kitchen and reached for a *bobosangbo*, the sack used to carry heavy loads on your back. She gathered three *sangbo* that kept bowls warm and food safe from flies. Ji-su bowed before Buddha's altar, as her mother had taught her. She lifted the *majibo*, a food offering cloth, folded next to Buddha's statue. Ji-su and Gomo looked at the different fabrics, seams, and stitches.

After her chores the next day, Ji-su set out scraps left over from when Eomma sewed short jackets called *jeogori*, the high-waisted skirts called *chima*, and the family's winter quilts. She arranged fabrics on the floor, like dogwood petals on the ground.

"Feel the fabrics," Gomo said. "Ramie, light and easy to stitch. Cotton, cool in summer and warm when quilted for winter. Hemp, strong like an iron kettle. Choose fabrics of the same weight and place them in matching piles." Gomo continued. "Colors should blend like blues in the sky and yellows of the sunrise over mountains or contrast like purple and gold in iris flowers."

Ji-su chose pomegranate red and pine green. She remembered how long and crooked her stitches were when she was only six and first learning to sew by following Eomma's basting threads. Now, Ji-su ripped out what she had sewn and practiced with smaller and more even stitches while Gomo quietly chanted.

After many weeks, Jisu held up her first *bojagi* for Gomo to see. "I made this all myself."

Hibiscus bloomed in the garden. Spring turned to summer. Ji-su's cousins played while Ji-su worked on a *bojagi* with the colors of summer fruit: peach, plum and cherry. Each tiny stitch felt like a step closer to Eomma.

In autumn, Ji-su's girl cousins played on the swing. Once she left her sewing to join them, hoping to see the trees on the other side of the wall instead of just the crowns of the trees like mushrooms peeking over the fence. Ji-su secretly promised herself to see what was beyond the wall someday. Gold and orange leaves danced in the wind, and Ji-su dreamed of the colors lining the path to Eomma.

One evening a bat flew under the eave. Ji-su touched a small knotted-bat sewn inside her *jeogori*. "Eomma sewed bats on her *bojagi* to bring good luck and keep evil spirits away."

"Watch how she made them." Gomo threaded a needle.

Day after day Ji-su knotted delicate fabrics until she had a colorful pile of bats in her lap. Gomo picked up one. "These are as fine as Eomma's."

"I'll send Eomma wishes of happiness with blue bats," Ji-su whispered to Gomo. "Chung Ho is helping Uncle deliver pomegranates to the palace soon. I will give him a *bojagi* for Eomma."

"The king's palace has many buildings," Gomo said. "Chung Ho can take it, but it may not get to Eomma."

Eomma, be safe. Ji-su sent a message with each stitch on fine cotton scraps. Eomma be well. Eomma, be happy. Her wrapping cloth grew each day while she kept her eye on persimmons dangling over the courtyard wall. She finished her last stitches, tiny and evenly spaced like Eomma's, just in time to catch Chung Ho leaving.

"I hope Eomma sends a *bojagi* back so I know she received mine," Ji-su told him.

But Chung Ho returned empty-handed.

When the New Year approached, Ji-su's cousins played *yut*, her favorite game, but instead she sewed.

One day Ji-su ran to Gomo. "Chung Ho told me the Sanguiwon master will arrive in one month. I will sew my best *bojagi* before the full moon rises so the Sanguiwon master will choose me to sew with Eomma in King Yongjo's court."

"It must be your finest work," Gomo said.

Ji-su fit odd-shaped pieces of ramie together like a puzzle. She made every stitch tight and perfect. The *bojagi* grew along with her dream of being with Eomma again. When the full moon rose, Ji-su hurried to attach a blue bat.

When Chung Ho told her the Sanguiwon master had arrived, Ji-su walked to the gate, trembling.

Ji-su bowed low as she presented her wrapping cloth. The Sanguiwon master nodded at the design, examined the stitches, and checked each seam. "One of our finest seamstresses showed me a *bojagi* this fine." He turned to his assistant. "Are there more *bojagi* by this woman?"

"I have more," Ji-su murmured.

He studied the blue bat. "You couldn't have made this."

"I did. Wait," whispered Ji-su, bowing. She ran to her room and gathered her other *bojagi*.

The Sanguiwon master examined each one. "No, not as good," he said. "Uneven stitches, crooked seams, and uncut threads. Each *bojagi* must be perfect." He tossed the pile down.

Bowing, Ji-su stepped back. "I meant to leave my red and green *bojagi* in my drawer."

"Even the Sanguiwon master knows everyone must start as a beginner." Gomo took Ji-su's hand. The Sanguiwon master glared at Gomo, then mounted his horse and rode off.

"I'll never see Eomma again," Ji-su whispered.

"You did your best and that is enough."

Hours passed, and Ji-su didn't eat
the *kimchi* or *mandoo* Gomo brought.
Her favorite fermented vegetables
and dumplings couldn't comfort her.

News of the Sanguiwon
master leaving spread through the
village. Ji-su wept.

But before he left, the
Sanguiwon master summoned
Ji-su. "Show me the *bojagi* with
the blue bat again." He studied
each seam. "If you can make
one as fine as this before the
Dano Festival, I will look at it
as I pass through."

Ji-su began again. Nothing else mattered.
Cousins watched from the door before Gomo shooed
them away. Aunts commented on Ji-su's most intricate
design. Flowers on the dogwood tree bloomed and peonies
opened.

One evening, Ji-su gasped at a red spot on the fabric. She
searched her fingers and found blood smeared on one tip, rubbed
raw from pushing the needle. Ji-su ripped out the stained stitches and
rinsed the cloth.

Preparations began for Dano,
a festival marking the completion of
planting the fields. Children practiced for the
swinging, seesawing, and wrestling contests. Ji-su's aunts prepared rice
cakes. After boiling Sweet Flag, a plant with scented leaves, women washed
their hair with the special water in the hope of preventing misfortune. Ji-su rinsed
her hair twice.

The day before the festival, Ji-su added the final
stitch. She wondered if the Sanguiwon master
forgot his promise to return.

When lanterns were lit, Ji-su heard
horses trotting. Voices and dust rose near
the courtyard gate.

"Ji-su, you've been summoned,"
Gomo called. "Bring your *bojagi*."

Kneeling in her lowest bow, Ji-su presented her *bojagi*. "For you."

Examining it, the Sanguiwon master nodded. From his pouch he took the first *bojagi* she had given him, and then another one. Her heart leaped against her chest and her legs felt weak at the sight of the *bojagi* she sent her mother so long ago.

"When I saw your *bojagi*, I did not think a young girl could do work this fine. A sewing woman in the palace said her daughter had sewn this one. She wanted to keep it, but I brought it with me to find the girl who sewed it." He handed Ji-su all her *bojagi*. "You must be the daughter. You are chosen to sew for the king. Be ready at sunrise."

The next morning, quick good-byes to aunts and
cousins felt like clipping threads. Ji-su tied her few
possessions in her largest *bojagi*. She saved the one she
made for Eomma to give to her. Ji-su handed Gomo the
last one. "Thank you for all you taught me."

"It was an honor."
Gomo held Ji-su close.
"Now you will be
with Eomma."

Ji-su walked through winding, mountainous paths for
three days toward King Yongjo's court. Following the curve
in the road, Ji-su remembered her dreams
of going on this path toward
Eomma. Ji-su wished the
escorts would go faster.

In a small palace courtyard Ji-su saw a woman's shadow. The door slid open.

"Eomma!" Ji-su hurried to her.

"My dear daughter." Eomma and Ji-su held each other like threads in a seam.

Ji-su opened her *bojagi*.

Eomma examined it. "Each stitch has brought us together again."

Ji-su nodded. "Good fortune is in a wrapping cloth."

Glossary

bobusangbo (BOH-boo-sahng-boh): a cloth sack used by merchants to carry their goods

bojagi (BOH-jah-ghee): a square, hemmed cloth of various sizes, colors, and designs

bok (bohk): good fortune

chima (CHEE-mah): a long wrap-around skirt for women and girls

Dano (DAHN-oh) Festival: a celebration marking the end of planting season held on the fifth day of the fifth month of the lunar calendar

darimi (DAH-ree-mee): an iron with a flat-bottomed bowl to hold hot charcoal

Eomma (UHM-ma): Mother

indoo (EEN-doo): a small iron with a long wooden handle

jeogori (JUH-goh-ree): a short jacket with long ties worn by women and girls

kimchi (GHEEM-chee): a fermented vegetable dish

majibo (MAH-jee-boh): a *bojagi* to wrap food offerings to Buddha

mandoo (MAHN-doo): dumplings

sangbo (SAHNG-boh): a *bojagi* used as a tablecloth

Sanguiwon (SAHNG-ee-wuhn) master: overseer of the sewing needs of a palace

Yut (yoot): a Korean board game

Author's Notes

I was inspired to write this story after viewing a collection of *bojagi*, Korean wrapping cloths, on display at the Asian Art Museum in San Francisco. *Bojagi*, sewn by women, held an important place in the everyday lives of all classes of Koreans during the Joseon Dynasty (1392-1897). They were used for everything from storing foods and household items to covering bedding and screens, and wrapping gifts. Before the advent of paper and plastic for protecting and transporting items, *bojagi* were a sensible way to fill many needs in society.

Artistic creativity was embraced in *bojagi*. Women used scraps of fabrics to create works of art. Abstract designs, contrasting or complementing colors, and intricate stitches and embroidery are evident in their wrapping cloths. Sewing was an important aspect of the lives of Korean women. Common women often worked alone in their rooms creating these artistic designs.

Koreans believed good luck could be enclosed within a *bojagi*. Blessings and good wishes accompanied each stitch and piece of fabric. Also, wrapping a gift in a *bojagi* offered blessings of good luck and happiness to the receiver. Weddings, birthdays, and New Year's celebrations offered opportunities to share gifts wrapped in *bojagi*.

Shown are two examples of *bojagi*. The *subo*, or embroidered *bojagi*, shows exquisite handiwork on decorated cloth. The *chogak bo*, or patchwork *bojagi*, is made from scraps of material left over after sewing. They are similar to patchwork quilts found in the West.

Images courtesy of the San Francisco Asian Art Museum

"To Peg, remembering all she did for me" — *J.S.*
"To Rose" — *J.L.*

Author Acknowledgments:

I am grateful to Chunghie Lee, a Korean-born fiber artist known internationally for her artwork, for inspiring me to write this after viewing some of her *bojagi* and for sharing her expertise on wrapping cloths. A special thanks to John Stucky, museum librarian at the San Francisco Asian Art Museum, Yeonsoo Chee, curator at the Pacific Asian Museum in Pasadena, and the librarians at the Fresno County Library for supportive research. A special thank you to the many Korean people in Fresno who invited me into their homes, lent books, and shared their culture, and to Bob for his unwavering support.

Book design and production by Patty Arnold, *www.menageriedesign.net*

Library of Congress Cataloging-in-Publication Data

Schoettler, Joan.

Good fortune in a wrapping cloth / by Joan Schoettler ; illustrated by Jessica Lanan.

   p. cm.

Summary: When Ji-su's mother is chosen by the emperor to be a seamstress in his court, Ji-su vows to learn to sew the beautiful Korean bojagi, or wrapping cloths, just as well so that she will also be summoned to the palace and be reunited with her mother.

ISBN 978-1-885008-40-4

[1. Wrapping cloths--Fiction. 2. Sewing--Fiction. 3. Perseverance (Ethics)--Fiction. 4. Mothers and daughters--Fiction. 5. Korea--History--18th century--Fiction.] I. Lanan, Jessica, ill. II. Title.

PZ7.S367Go 2011

[E]--dc22

2011001702

SHEN'S BOOKS

SHEN'S BOOKS
Walnut Creek, California
Sharing a World of Stories
888-456-6660
www.shens.com